Wonderland

Written By

Tommy Kovac

Illustrated by

Sonny Liew

Disney PRESS

New York

Printed in Singapore

First Edition
1 3 5 7 9 10 8 6 4 2

Library of Congress Control Number on file.

ISBN: 978-1-44231-0451-3

Visit www.disneybooks.com

Table of Contents

Chapter One
Impostor!

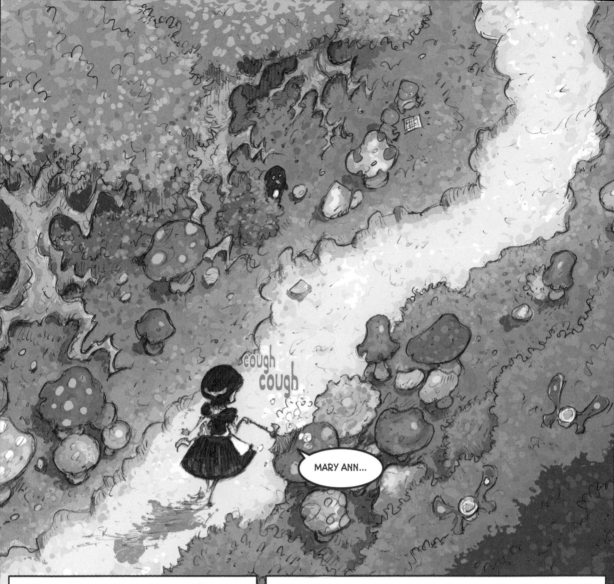

MARY ANN!

OH, SORRY, FEATHER.

SIGH

IT'S JUST THAT I'M RUNNING LATE AND BOUND TO GET A LECTURE FROM MASTER RABBIT.

YOU'RE LATE BECAUSE YOU SPENT SO MUCH TIME BLEACHING, STARCHING, AND IRONING THIS APRON!

THERE WAS A SPOT!

IT WAS A *SHADOW.*

ABOUT SOMEONE IN YOUR OWN SERVICE, YOUR RADIANCE!

WHAAAAAT?!!

WHAT... DID... YOU... SAY...??

IT'S TRUE! IT HAS TO DO WITH THE ALICE MONSTER!

WE DO NOT *SPEAK* OF THAT THING. WE ARE STILL CLEANING UP THE MESS THAT THING MADE IN THE ROYAL COURTROOM.

BUT PLEASE, DO GO ON.

I'D HATE TO THINK HE WAS ANYTHING BUT A NICE LOYAL BUNNY RABBIT, BUT IT WAS SHORTLY AFTER THEIR MEETING THAT THE MONSTER GOT SO DREADFULLY, ILLEGALLY HUGE AND WRECKED THE QUEEN'S BEE-YOOTIFUL COURTROOM...

SUCH A SHAME!

HE WAS CONSPIRING AGAINST ME? MY VERY OWN HERALD?

GUARDS!

OFF WITH HIS HEAD!

OFF WITH THE HEAD OF THE TRAITOR!!!

OH, I DO NOT LIKE BEING A TATTLETALE.

ME, NEITHER! MMM, LET'S HAVE SOME MORE OF THAT CUSTARD THING...

I'M VERY SORRY, MASTER RABBIT, IT'S TERRIBLY STUPID OF ME.

WE RUN A TIGHT SHIP HERE, MARY ANN! IT'S BECAUSE OF THIS SORT OF IRRESPONSIBILITY THAT YOU'LL NEVER RISE TO THE SORT OF STATUS AND POSITION *I* ENJOY.

I PRIDE MYSELF ON BEING PROMPT AND DEPENDABLE FOR THE QUEEN. I'D NEVER *DREAM* OF BEING LATE!

OR SH-SH-SHE'D HAVE MY *HEAD*!

HERE ARE YOUR GLOVES, MASTER RABBIT.

MY GLOVES, YES.

DID I ASK FOR MY GLOVES?

19

I ASSUME YOU'LL BE WANTING THEM, SINCE YOU'RE GOING OUT.

ER... YES.

GOING OUT?

WELL, SIR, YOU'RE DUE AT YOUR POST IN THE QUEEN'S CHAMBERS IN THREE MINUTES.

OH, WHY OF COURSE--

THREE MINUTES?!!

TICK TOCK, TICK TOCK, BUNNY RABBIT!

BUT I WOULDN'T BOTHER RUSHING TO THE QUEEN'S SIDE. SHE'S ON HER WAY HERE RIGHT NOW.

HERE?! WHY HERE?!

DO I HAVE TIME TO POLISH THE SILVER?!

SEEMS YOU'VE BEEN INCRIMINATED, BUNNY-RABBIT. FOR SUSPICIOUS DEALINGS WITH THE ALICE MONSTER...

BUT, I--

MONSTER? WHAT'S THIS ABOUT?

WHILE YOU WERE GONE, THERE WAS AN IMPOSTOR HERE! SHE WRECKED SOME OF THE ROOMS, AND SHOT THE GROUNDS-KEEPER OUT OF THE CHIMNEY LIKE A PEA OUT OF A PEASHOOTER.

I THOUGHT SHE WAS YOU AT FIRST!

THOUGHT SHE WAS ME?

WELL, SHE WAS A GIRL LIKE YOU, AND WAS WEARING SOME SORT OF DRESS, AND SHE HAD SOME SORT OF HAIR ON HER HEAD-- I DON'T KNOW!

I SUPPOSE I WAS DISTRACTED AT THE TIME.

AM I THAT NONDESCRIPT?

I KNOW I'M JUST A MAID, BUT...

BONG!

BONG!

BONG!

TIME'S UP, RABBIT! YOUR DAYS OF FAVOR WITH THE QUEEN ARE OVER!

RABBIT!!!

BANG

OH, YOUR MAJESTY! WHY, IT'S SO NICE OF YOU TO COME BY MY HUMBLE ABODE!

I'LL GET THE TEA THINGS...

NOBODY MOVE!

DEEEEEEAR RABBIT, I JUST WANTED TO HAVE A *WORD* WITH YOU. JUST A TEENY, TINY, *DAINTY* LITTLE WORD.

NO NEED TO RUN AROUND LIKE A RABBIT WITH ITS HEAD ABOUT TO BE CUT OFF.

JUST TELL ME EXACTLY WHAT YOU WERE DOING CONSPIRING WITH THE ALICE MONSTER.

OH, IT'S NOT TRUE! I NEVER! I DON'T! I WOULDN'T! I HAVE *NOT*!

REEEEEEEEALLY...

THEN *WHAT* IS THIS *GIANT STRAND* OF *LONG BLOND HAIR* DOING IN YOUR HOUSE?!!

TRAITOR!!!

25

Chapter Two
The Tulgey Wood & the Treacle Well

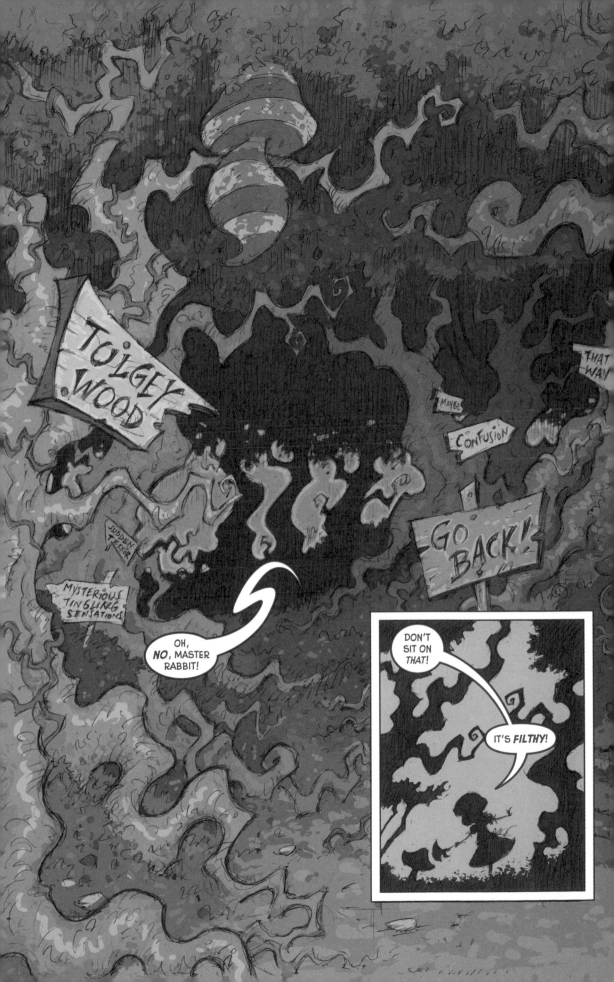

HERE, SIT ON **THIS** ONE. I'VE CLEANED IT THOROUGHLY.

wheeze!

TOO THOROUGHLY!

OH, WHAT AM I TO **DO**!? IF I SHOW MY FUZZY EARS AND WHISKERS OUTSIDE OF THIS DREADFUL FOREST, THE QUEEN WILL HAVE MY **HEAD**!

YES, IT DOES LOOK THAT WAY, SIR. BUT NOT BEFORE SHE LOPS **MINE** OFF.

YOURS? WHY, THE QUEEN DOESN'T EVEN KNOW YOUR **NAME**, GIRL! YOU'RE JUST A SERVANT, AND IN THIS CASE, THAT KEEPS YOU SAFE!

A SERVANT I MAY BE, BUT I KNOCKED THE QUEEN STRAIGHT OUT OF HER SENSES! FLAT ON HER BACK! SHE'LL BE ASKING AROUND FOR ME, SURE ENOUGH.

OH, THERE *MUST* BE SOME WAY FOR ME TO GET BACK ON HER *GOOD* SIDE...

I'M SURE I'M DOOMED, MASTER RABBIT--

SURELY *SOME* OF YOUR FRIENDS AND ACQUAINTANCES MUST KNOW MY NAME?

YOU MUST HAVE MENTIONED IT?

OH, I DON'T THINK SO. IT WOULDN'T BE VERY GENTEEL TO TALK ABOUT THE HELP LIKE THAT.

NO, I THINK YOU'RE FAIRLY SAFE, MARY ANN. WITH YOUR NONDESCRIPT LOOKS IT WILL BE EASY FOR *YOU* TO JUST--

THAT'S IT! WE'LL HIDE OUT AT *YOUR* HOUSE!

THE QUEEN WOULD NEVER EVEN KNOW WHERE TO LOOK! I MEAN, *I* DON'T EVEN KNOW WHERE YOU LIVE! I COULD FIGURE OUT A WAY TO INGRATIATE MYSELF ONCE AGAIN...

OH, NO, SIR! I DON'T THINK YOU'D BE VERY COMFORTABLE AT MY PLACE, SIR. I MEAN, IT'S A ROTTEN, DODGY KIND OF PLACE, COMPARED TO WHAT YOU ARE *USED* TO.

35

OH. WELL... I'M SURE I COULD ADAPT TO IT.

TEMPORARILY, OF COURSE.

EH-- HOW BAD *IS* IT?

OH, IT'S HORRIBLE, MASTER RABBIT. IT'S BUT A ONE-ROOM SHACK!

SURROUNDED BY SLOWSAND, TOO, SIR!

SLOWSAND?

OH, YES! YOU KNOW, INSTEAD OF QUICKSAND, WHICH SUCKS YOU RIGHT DOWN INTO IT, WITH SLOWSAND IF YOU EVEN *TOUCH* IT, IT PUTS YOU IN SLOW MOTION FOR HOURS.

WOULD TAKE YOU 20 MINUTES JUST TO SAY YOUR NAME.

OH, D-D-DEAR! HOW DO YOU CROSS IT, THEN?

WELL, YOU HAVE TO STEP ACROSS THE BACKS OF THE TURTLES WHO LIVE IN THE SLOWSAND.

AND THEN THERE'S THE TEETERING ROCK.

TEETERING...?

YES. A HUGE ROCK PERCHED PRECARIOUSLY ON AN OVERHANG DIRECTLY ABOVE THE SHACK. TEETERING, YOU KNOW? YOU HAVE TO BE *VERY QUIET* AT ALL TIMES. OTHERWISE...

SMASH!

OH. WELL. I SEE. YES, OF COURSE. PERHAPS YOUR HOUSE ISN'T THE BEST PLACE TO GO AT THE MOMENT...

OH, THE INSIDE IS IMMACULATE AND TIDY, OF COURSE, BUT IT'S STILL A MISERABLE, SORRY, LITTLE HOVEL, SIR.

MASTER RABBIT...?

DO YOU HEAR THAT STRANGE... SINGING?

SOUNDS MORE LIKE *CATERWAULING* TO ME...

IT SOUNDS A BIT FAMILIAR... I CAN ALMOST PLACE IT...

B-B-BAD LUCK?!

YES, SIR. IT'S A TERRIBLE CURSE TO RECITE *THAT* POEM IN *THIS* WOOD! EVERY-BODY KNOWS THAT!

OH, IT'S JUST A HARMLESS LITTLE RHYME. RIGHT, BUNNY RABBIT?

WELL, OF COURSE! JUST A *SILLY* RHYME AND NOTHING MORE!

BEGGING YOUR PARDON, MASTER RABBIT, BUT YOU *CAN'T* SAY *THAT* POEM IN THE TULGEY WOOD, OR... OR...

TERRIBLE THINGS WILL HAPPEN!

THE *MONSTER* WILL COME!

OH, THAT'S PURE STUFF AND NONSENSE! JUST PEASANT SUPERSTITION.

IT'S **SO NICE** TO BE IN THE PRESENCE OF SUCH AN **INTELLECT**, BUNNY RABBIT.

SO **VERY** REFRESHING TO SEE YOU AREN'T FRIGHTENED BY SUCH FOOLISH, LOWER-CLASS BELIEFS.

YES, WELL. KNOWLEDGE IS POWER AND ALL THAT.

SO GO AHEAD.

HM? WHAT?

WELL, IF YOU DON'T BELIEVE THE LEGEND, THEN GO AHEAD AND RECITE THE POEM.

WELL... I...

OH, **DON'T**, MASTER RABBIT, SIR!

WHAT'S THE MATTER?

HM?

WHAT?

... DID GYRE AND GIMBLE IN THE WABE: ALL MIMSY WERE THE BOROGOVES, AND- THE-MOME-RATHS-OUTGRABE *OKAY YOU CAN SEE I KNOW THE STUPID POEM!*

WELL, AT LEAST YOU KNOW THE FIRST STANZA, WHICH I SUPPOSE IS IMPRESSIVE.

FOR A RABBIT.

BEWARE THE JABBERWOCK, MY SON! THE JAWS THAT BITE, THE CLAWS THAT CATCH! BEWARE THE JUBJUB BIRD, AND SHUN THE FRUMIOUS BANDERSNATCH!

OH, MASTER RABBIT, THAT'S *LOVELY*, AND A *VERY* GOOD RECITATION, BUT I'M SURE THAT'S ENOUGH TO--

I'D CERTAINLY UNDERSTAND IF YOU WANT TO STOP THERE, SINCE THE NEXT STANZA HAS MORE WORDS THAT MIGHT BE *DIFFICULT* FOR YOU TO PRONOUNCE, AND WE WOULDN'T WANT YOU TO BE *EMBARRASSED*--

YES, THAT'S VERY GOOD, BUNNY RABBIT.

HE TOOK HIS VORPAL SWORD IN HIS HAND: LONG TIME THE MANXOME FOE HE SOUGHT-- SO RESTED HE BY THE TUMTUM TREE, AND STOOD AWHILE IN THOUGHT.

GASP! I JUST FELT A BREATH! A HOT BREATH ON THE BACK OF MY NECK! I SWEAR IT!

SQUAWK! SOMETHING'S COMING! *SOMETHING'S COMING!!!* *SQUAWK!*

AND, AS IN UFFISH THOUGHT HE STOOD...

THE J-J-JABBERWOCK...

WITH EYES OF FLAME...

... WOOD--

CAME WH-WH-WHIFFLING THROUGH THE T-T-TULGEY...

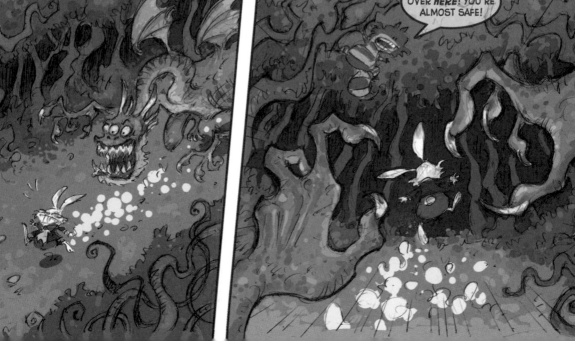

HUFF! HUFF!

WHEW!

MASTER RABBIT...?

MASTER RABBIT!

SHH! THE MONSTER'LL HEAR YOU!

BUT WHERE IS MASTER RABBIT? HE COULD BE IN *DREADFUL* TROUBLE!

OH, HE'S PROBABLY BEEN EATEN BY NOW. LET'S TAKE THAT AS OUR CUE TO--

OH, DEAR! WE'VE GOT TO GO BACK! POOR, CLUMSY, FOOLISH MASTER RABBIT! HE CAN'T TELL HIS HEAD FROM A HOLE IN THE GROUND, EVEN A *RABBIT HOLE*.

HE'LL BE NEEDING OUR HELP!

MARY ANN, HAS IT NOT OCCURRED TO YOU, YET, THAT THE WHITE RABBIT NO LONGER HAS THE STATUS HE ONCE DID? HE HAS BEEN BRANDED A TRAITOR TO THE QUEEN.

WHY SHOULD YOU CONTINUE TO SERVE HIS EVERY WHIM AND FANCY? THIS IS YOUR CHANCE TO LOOK FOR SOMETHING BETTER...

OH, I COULDN'T. I COULDN'T JUST ABANDON HIM.

I MEAN, WHAT WOULD I DO?

WHAT WOULD I... BE?

OH! A WELL! THANK GOODNESS! I CAN DRAW SOME WATER AND CLEAN MY FACE UP, GET MY HAIR BACK IN ORDER!

TREACLE

DRAT! WOULDN'T YOU JUST KNOW IT'S A TREACLE WELL!

AN OLD, ABANDONED TREACLE WELL.

NO USE AT ALL, THOSE THINGS.

DO YOU... DO YOU HEAR... *VOICES?*

COMING FROM DOWN INSIDE THE WELL?

IT'S PROBABLY THAT MANGY *CAT* AGAIN.

I WOULDN'T GO NEAR IT.

SPRONGG

WHOOPS--

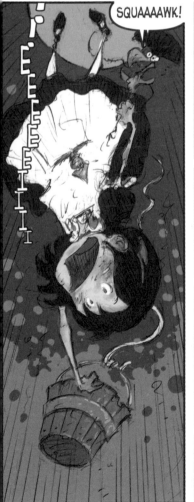

SQUAAAAWK!

FOOM

WELL, HOW QUEER!

I WONDER IF I'LL FALL RIGHT *THROUGH* THE--

WELCOME TO OUR COZY LITTLE HOME! WE *DO* LIKE TO SHARE IT, DON'T WE, GIRLS?

OH, MY GOODNESS, *YES!*

COME CLOSER, SWEETING! LET ME SMELL YOUR HAIR, IT LOOKS SO PRETTY...

IS... IS THERE A STRANGER HERE?

HAS SOMEONE COME FOR ME...?

OH, CRUMPET, WHAT A TREAT! YOU MUST COME IN AND MEET *SIR* AND *MADAME!* THEY'RE DELIGHTFUL COMPANY...

OH!

I BELIEVE THIS BELONGS TO YOU...

I... I DARE SAY IT DOES.

I KNOW FROM EXPERIENCE HOW MUCH THAT *SMARTS!*

OFF WITH HIS HEAD!

WAIT, WAIT, OFF WITH *ITS* HEAD, *FIRST!*

OFF WITH THE HEAD OF THE JABBERWOCK!!!

YES! YES THAT'S IT! THAT'S HOW TO VANQUISH THE BEAST!

"One, two! One, two! And through and through
The vorpal blade went snicker-snack!
He left it dead, and with its head
He went galumphing back."

I SAID *OFF WITH ITS HEAD*!!! WHAT ARE YOU FOOLS WAITING FOR?!

AND PUT MY HUSBAND DOWN THIS INSTANT!

OH, IT'S SHOCKING! IT'S BRUTAL! SURE IT WAS A BEAST, BUT SUCH SAVAGERY IS JUST *APPALLING!*

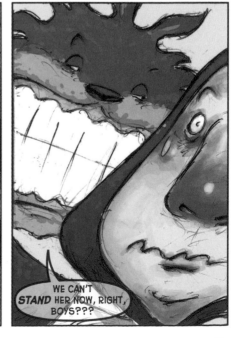

WE CAN'T *STAND* HER NOW, RIGHT, BOYS???

OH, FOR HEAVEN'S SAKE! IT'S JUST A PAGE FROM A DUSTY OLD BOOK OF ANTIQUE POETRY!

GASP!

HURRAH!!!

CLOD-FEARING SIMPLETONS...

NOW, ABOUT THAT RABBIT.

OFF WITH HIS HEAD!!!

HURRAH FOR THE QUEEN OF HEARTS!!!

"... LONG LIVE THE QUEEN!!!"

THANK YOU FOR RETURNING MY SCEPTER TO ME, YOUNG MAID.

YOU'RE MOST WELCOME... MA'AM? YOUR *GRACE*? YOUR... *HIGHNESS*?

'SCUSE ME FOR SAYING, YOU SEEM SOMEHOW... FAMILIAR. DO I KNOW YOU?

YOU'RE VERY YOUNG, BUT YOU MAY HAVE HEARD WHISPERS OF ME, FROM THOSE WHO KNEW ME BEFORE I CAME TO BE TRAPPED DOWN HERE IN THIS TREACLE WELL WITH... THE SISTERS.

I WAS ONCE THE QUEEN OF SPADES, OF COURSE.

OH! I COULD **TELL** YOU WERE A ROYAL!

I'M CALLED MARY ANN, YOUR MAJESTY, JUST A SIMPLE MAIDSERVANT TO THE WHITE RABBIT. AND I JUST WANT YOU TO KNOW THAT I AM A CLEAN, **TIDY** SORT OF GIRL, WHEN I DON'T HAPPEN TO BE AT THE BOTTOM OF A TREACLE WELL!

A STARCHED-LINENS, SCRUBBED-BEHIND-THE-EARS SORT OF GIRL! WHY, SCRUB MR. RABBIT'S FLOORS **THREE TIMES A DAY**, I DO, YOUR MAJESTY!

AND MY PERSONAL APPEARANCE IS SOMETHING I TAKE **VERY** SERIOUSLY, YOUR MAJESTY. **TRULY** I DO.

OOOH, LET'S MAKE HER UP ALL PRETTY!

A SEAWEED AND TREACLE PRINCESS!

DO LET ME SLIME YOUR HAIR FOR YOU, MY **WITTLE WEEDLING**...

A PROPER LADY-IN-WAITING IS QUIET AND POLITE. WHEN SHE *MUST* SPEAK SHE DOES SO *SOFTLY* AND KEEPS HER MOUTH MOSTLY *SHUT*.

HAVE THE DECENCY TO LOOK AT THE GROUND AND TWIDDLE YOUR FINGERS NERVOUSLY.

WHEN I CALL FOR *SILENCE*, YOU SHALL BRING ME BUSHELS AND CARTLOADS OF IT.

I WISH TO ACQUIRE GREAT *STOREHOUSES* OF SILENCE SO THAT I NEVER RUN OUT OF IT.

NOW LOOK AT YOUR DRESS.

IT IS SPOTLESSLY CLEAN.

LIKEWISE YOUR MOUTH.

OH, *THANK YOU!*

-- I MEAN, THANK YOU, YOUR MAJESTY!

71

OFF WITH HIS HEAD!

YES, MUM-- I MEAN YES, YOUR MAJESTY!

CHOP IT RIGHT OFF, WE WILL! RIGHT AWAY, YOUR BRILLIANCE!

OH, N-N-NO! NOT MY HEAD! MY POOR, FUZZY, LITTLE HEAD

HUSH, NOW!

YEAH, KEEP IT DOWN!

WE DON'T HAVE THE STOMACHS OR BEHEADINGS ANY MORE THAN *YOU* DO! JUST KEEP YOUR VOICE DOWN, SO'S THE QUEEN DON'T CATCH ON!

OH! ARE YOU GOING TO LET ME GO?! I WON'T SAY A WORD! I'M SO GRATEFUL! SO VERY, VERY--

WE AIN'T LETTIN' YOU *GO*, BUNNY-RABBIT. THE QUEEN WOULD HAVE *OUR* HEADS.

WE'RE JUST DISPOSIN' OF YOU ELSEWHERES...

DISPOSING OF ME?! OH, NO, PLEASE! I DON'T WISH TO BE AT YOUR DISPOSAL!

I'M INDISPOSABLE! OH, **HELP!**

NO, NO! NOT DOWN *THERE!*

WHY DOES YOUR HUSBAND SAY NOTHING?

HE IS MY *MATE*. WE SHARE OUR THOUGHTS, OUR DREAMS, OUR OPINIONS, OUR VOICE...

AND RIGHT NOW *I'M* USING *ALL* THOSE THINGS.

OH, YES. OF COURSE.

IT SEEMS A LONG AND SLIPPERY CLIMB...

ISN'T EVERYTHING?

WE'D BE SURE TO BREAK OUR NECKS...

UNDOUBTEDLY!

WELL, *YOU* WOULD, *I* CAN FLY.

BUT STILL, THERE MUST BE *SOME* WAY TO--

AAAAAAAA

AAUGH!

SPLOOSH

OH, D-D-*DEAR!*

WHY, IT'S THE QUEEN OF SPADES! YOUR MAJESTY! SO **THIS** IS WHERE YOU DIS-APPEARED TO!

EXCUSE ME, MARY ANN.

THANKS TO YOUR MISTRESS, THE QUEEN OF HEARTS, WHO TOSSED US DOWN HERE.

I SEEM TO REMEMBER YOU AS HER HERALD TOOTLING ON THAT ANNOYING TRUMPET WELL, YOU'RE NOTHIN NOW, RABBIT. YOU'V BEEN BROUGHT LOW--

LITERALLY!

YOU AND YOUR **FORMER** MAIDSERVANT ARE **MY** SUBJECTS, NOW.

OH, YES, MA'AM, OF COURSE I UNDERSTA--

STOP. STOP THAT. **STOP IT**! STOP **PETTING** ME, YOU GHOULS, I'M NOT A POODLE!

THIS IS QUITE INSULTING!

CHOOO!

CHOOO!

MISTER BUTTERFLY, SIR! THIS IS PERFECT!

IT IS NOT.

OH, PLEASE, SIR! WE'RE THE PERFECT SIZE FOR YOU TO CARRY US OUT OF THE WELL!

I WILL NOT.

YOU *WILL*, OR WHEN I HAVE REGAINED MY STATURE, I SHALL ORDER YOU *PINNED*.

I SHALL BE HAPPY TO ASSIST YOU.

I SHALL EXPECT SOME SORT OF ENTERTAINMENT TO BE PROVIDED DURING OUR FLIGHT.

THE YOUNG MISS SHOULD RECITE A POEM...

OH, I NEVER LEARNT ANYTHING FUN OR FRIVOLOUS AS A POEM. BUT I COULD RECITE INSTRUCTIONS ON HOW TO GET HAIR-OIL STAINS OUT OF AN ANTIMACASSAR.

IT WILL HAVE TO DO.

Chapter Four
The Curious

THANKS FOR THE LIFT. THAT WAS RIGHT KIND OF YOU, SIR!

YOU'RE WELCOME, MISS. AT LEAST *SOMEONE* HAS MANNERS.

OH *MY!* WE ARE HONORED TO BE HOSTING *ROYALTY* AT OUR HUMBLE TABLE!

THERE'LL BE TROUBLE WHEN THE QUEEN OF HEARTS GETS A GANDER AT *THEM!*

THIS IS LOVELY, YOU'RE ALL *JUST* IN TIME FOR TEA!

I SHOULD LIKE A BITTER, *BLACK* TEA, AND A VERY HARD, *DRY* SCONE.

AND SOME TREACLE, PERHAPS?

ABSO*LUTE*LY NOT!

WHAT ABOUT TEA FOR *HIM?*

HE'S SICK FROM TOO MUCH TREACLE. JUST POUR THE TEA INTO HIS CROWN, AND HE'LL ABSORB IT THROUGH HIS SCALP.

HERE, MARY ANN, SIT NEXT TO ME AND I'LL HELP YOU WITH THE ETIQUET REQUIRED AT A TEA PARTY. NOW, WHE THEY SERVE THE FIRST COURSE, YOU'LL PICK UP THIS—

EWWW!!

HORRORS!

MISTER HATTER, SIR? I'M SORRY TO BE A PROBLEM, BUT THESE TEA THINGS SEEM TO BE DIRTY. THERE'S EVEN A *MOUSE* IN THE TEAPOT!

MAY I HAVE A CLEAN—

MOVE DOWN! CLEAN CUP! MOVE DOWN!

BUT THIS PLACE ISN'T CLEAN, EITHER. MASTER RABBIT WAS JUST SITTING HERE!

WE MOVED *COUNTER* CLOCKWISE, THEREFORE YOU'RE ACTUALLY SITTING AT THAT PLACE *BEFORE* HE DID.

YOUR MAJESTY'S HANDMAID IS REALLY QUITE DENSE WHEN IT COMES TO PHYSICS!

OH, BLIMEY, SOMEONE HAD BETTER TELL THE JAM AND THE TEA TO STOP FIDGETING, OR THE TABLECLOTH WILL BE RUINED!

SHHH! GET HOLD OF YOURSELF, MARY ANN!

SHRIEEEK!

IS IT THE QUEEN OF HEARTS?! HAS SHE COME FOR ME?!

I JUST *KNEW* IT-

YOU'RE JUST BEING SPITEFUL.

AT LEAST LET ME TAKE CARE OF SOME OF THESE CRUSTY DISHES WHERE NOBODY'S SITTING!

NOBODY WOULD CONSIDER THAT VERY RUDE, SEEING AS HOW HE'S STILL USING THEM!

IF YOU OFFEND NOBODY, YOUR REPUTATION WILL BE RUINED!

OH!

HONK

HANDMAID! STOP FUSSING, AND COME HERE INSTANTLY!

CUT MY TEA INTO BITE-SIZE SIPS!

I'LL BE THERE IN A MOMENT, YOUR MAJESTY, I JUST *HAVE* TO DO THIS WHILE I HAVE THE CHANCE!

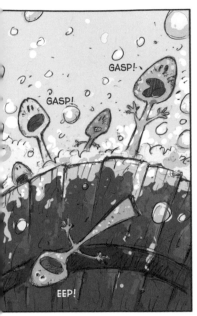

GASP!

GASP!

EEP!

NEVER MIND THE SPOONS, YOU'VE SCRUBBED THE PATTERNS RIGHT OFF THE CHINA!

HERE THEY ARE! IN THE DISH WATER!

TRiP

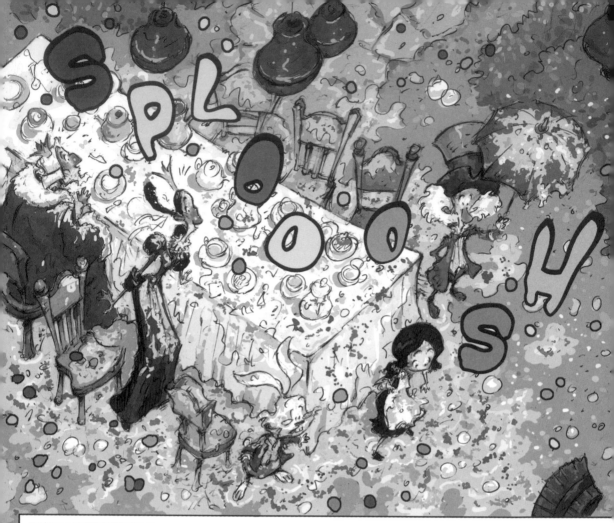

THIS WILL NEVER DO!

IT'S TIME WE MADE A VISIT TO SIR EDWARD THE TAILOR.

WE CANNOT BE DAMP, GARISH, AND SHABBY WHEN I CONFRONT MY BLOATED NEMESIS, THE QUEEN OF HEARTS.

COME ALONG!

I... I HAVE... AN OPINION!

YOU HAVE A *WHAT*?! HOW *DARE* YOU!

WHERE DID HE GET IT?

IS IT *DANGEROUS*?

HAVE ALL THE OPINIONS, AND I WILL NOT SHARE! I DEMAND YOU GIVE IT BACK TO ME, STRAIGHTAWAY!

YOU KNOW, WE HAD ANOTHER YOUNG LADY COME BY FOR TEA JUST A LITTLE WHILE AGO. THAT WAS *BEFORE* SHE OUTGREW HERSELF AND ENDED UP IN COURT. MIGHT YOU BE A FRIEND OF HERS?

SO! THE ALICE MONSTER WAS *HERE*, TOO, WAS SHE?

YOU KNOW, THEY SAY SHE'S BEEN SIGHTED IN *LOOKING-GLASS HOUSE*. BUT DON'T TELL THE QUEEN OF HEARTS!

SHE HAS *FOLLOWERS* NOW, WHO CALL THEMSELVES "THE CURIOUS."

WHY WOULD ANYONE FOLLOW A MONSTER?

THERE ARE THOSE WHO QUITE LIKED THE WAY SHE CALLED THE QUEEN'S GUARD "NOTHING BUT A PACK OF CARDS..."

AND SHE'S NOT AFRAID TO CALL "NONSENSE!" WHEN SHE SEES IT.

OH, POPPYCOCK! THAT WOULD BE LIKE YELLING "SKY!" EVERY TIME YOU LOOK UP!

I THINK THIS ALICE MONSTER SOUNDS MORE INTERESTING ALL THE TIME!

I THINK SHE SOUNDS TERRIBLE AND RUDE! IF EVERY GIRL WERE A *BACK-TALKING, STUCK-UP LITTLE PRAT*, WONDERLAND WOULD BE A JAGGED PLACE, INDEED!

YES, AND IT'S ALL BECAUSE OF THAT HORRID ALICE BEAST THAT I'VE BEEN ACCUSED OF TREASON!

OH, DEAR! *TREASON*, YOU SAY?! PERHAPS WE SHOULDN'T EVEN BE HAVING THIS LITTLE CHAT-

SO IT'S TRUE, CAT'S *DO* GROW ON TREES! WE MUST MAKE A NOTE OF THAT!

I'LL WRITE IT IN FROSTING, SO WE'LL NEVER FORGET!

NOW, AS I WAS SAYING, TEATIME IS OVER, SO YOU ALL REALLY MUST BE GOING!

WHAT?! TEATIME'S *NEVER* OVER HERE! ALL YOUR CLOCKS ARE STOPPED AT EXACTLY SIX O' CLOCK!

NOW, DON'T TRY TO INTIMIDATE ME WITH YOUR TRAITOROUS CRIMINAL CUNNING! PLEASE JUST GO ON YOUR WAY, AND WE'LL FORGET YOU WERE HERE!

THIS IS RIDICULOUS! YOU TWO HAD *TEA* WITH THE ALICE MONSTER! ALL *I* DID WAS-

COME HERE, RABBIT! WE HAVE MORE IMPORTANT THINGS TO DO!

IT'S JUST ALONG THE WAY HERE A BIT.

SIR EDWARD IS A FINE TAILOR AND A CLEVER DRESS-MAKER.

IT'S CRUEL NOT TO LET ME EAT YOU! YOU'VE BEEN STEEPED IN TEA AND SUGARED LIBERALLY.

YOU'RE THE *PERFECT SNACK!*

AH, YES, HERE WE ARE.

SIR EDWARD! WE HAVE NEED OF YOUR SERVICES!

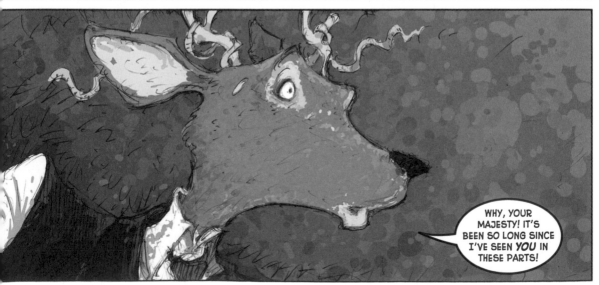

WHY, YOUR MAJESTY! IT'S BEEN SO LONG SINCE *YOU* IN THESE PARTS!

YOU DO LOOK *LOVELY*, MARY ANN.

LET ME JUST...

WHY, IT'S NOT DRAB AT ALL, IT'S—

OOF!

LOOSE ENDS MAKE ME NERVOUS. I PREFER CLOSURE.

YOU'VE HEMMED ME IN!

BUTTON YOUR LIP, GIRL, IT'S FOR YOUR OWN GOOD. WE CAN'T HAVE YOU FALLING OUT OF YOUR DRESS, NOW, CAN WE?

DO YOU ENJOY YOUR JOB, DEAR? WHAT I MEAN IS, DO YOU DERIVE ANY FULFILLMENT FROM IT?

I SUPPOSE SO, YES, SIR.

I MEAN, I'VE NEVER BEEN A *HANDMAID* BEFORE, BUT I SUPPOSE IT WON'T BE SO VERY DIFFERENT FROM BEING A HOUSEMAID.

HM, YES. HAVE YOU EXPERIENCE WITH HANDS? OR ARE YOU MOSTLY AN EXPERT ON HOUSES?

WELL, I DO HAVE SEVERAL HANDS OF MY OWN, SIR, AND I'M WELL ACQUAINTED WITH THEM. ALTHOUGH THEY'RE A DIFFERENT TYPE THAN THE QUEEN'S.

OH! GET AWAY!

I KNOW, THEY'RE SUCH A BOTHER.

HAVE YOU TRIED MOTH-BALLS?

YES, AND THEY WERE *GRAND* AFFAIRS, WITH MUSIC AND DANCING, BUT IT'S STILL NOT *ENOUGH* FOR THESE UNGRATEFUL FLIBBERTY-GIBBETS.

THEY'RE ALWAYS RIGHT BACK THE NEXT DAY, NIBBLING AWAY AT MY BEST FABRICS!

WELL, I MEAN THE *OTHER* SORT OF MOTHBALLS. I USE THEM ALL THE TIME FOR MASTER RABBIT'S THINGS.

OH, YOU'RE A SMART GIRL! I BET YOU HAVE ALL SORTS OF CLEVER METHODS!

WELL, I'M NOTHING SPECIAL, BUT I *DO* PRIDE MYSELF ON RUNNING A NEAT HOUSEHOLD.

I... I DON'T SUPPOSE YOU MIGHT BE NEEDING AN *ASSISTANT* HERE IN YOUR SHOP?

WELL, SIR EDWARD, I BELIEVE YOU'RE FINISHED WITH *MY HANDMAID* NOW.

GIRL, IT'S THE RABBIT'S TURN. PERHAPS YOU SHOULD TAKE A NICE STROLL IN THE GARDEN.

OUTSIDE.

SIGH

WH—WHERE IS IT?

THE CATERPILLAR? HE'S METAMOR-PHOSED.

WHERE IS WHAT?

THE C-C-CAT!

NO, NO, THE *CAT*! THE FUZZY MEAN ONE WITH THE TEETH!

OH, YOU MUST MEAN THE PUSSY WILLOWS! BUT THEY DON'T HAVE THORNS...

GROOWWWL...

IF I WERE IN YOUR PREDICAMENT, I WOULDN'T *HIDE* BEHIND THAT MUSHROOM, I'D *EAT* IT.

HM.
IT'S THAT HOUSE THE HARE MENTIONED...

LOOKING GLASS HOUSE

?

CURIOUSER...?

...

...

...AND CURIOUSER.

YOU MAY ENTER.

MARY ANN, COME LOOK!

WHAT IS EVERYONE GAWKING AT?

LOOK! IN THE GLASS... ON THE OTHER SIDE!

cough cough HACK

IS *THAT* THE ALICE MONSTER? HOW STRANGE...

I DREAMED ABOUT THAT GIRL!

Chapter Five
The Dusty Dunes

IN THE DREAM, IT WAS LIKE I SAW EVERYTHING THROUGH HER EYES...

EXCUSE ME, MISS! DO YOU KNOW ANYTHING 'BOUT THE RUMORS WHAT BEEN FLYING AROUND, 'BOUT THE ROYALS?

WE HEARD THE QUEEN OF SPADES TOOK HER O SCEPTER AND KNOCKED T QUEEN OF HEARTS FLAT ON HER FANNY!

IT WAS *MARY ANN* WHO DID THAT!

OH! ARE *YOU* THE QUEEN OF SPADES?

NO, I AM NOT!

WELL, YOU MUST BE FEARSOME AND POWERFUL, TO HAVE KNOCKED OUT THE QUEEN OF HEARTS!

OH, NO! I'M NOTHING LIKE THAT BEASTLY ALICE!

HERE WE THOUGHT *ALICE* WAS THE ONLY ONE WHAT KNEW HOW TO PUT THEM ROYALS IN THEIR PLACE!

YES, MISSY, CAN'T YOU PLEASE TEACH US HOW TO BE SMART AN' SASSY, TOO?

OH, BUT I THINK YOU ARE! YOU'RE A MOSTLY *HUMAN* GIRL, RIGHT? WITH ONE OF THEM GIRLY-TYPE FACES.

AND *HAIR!* DON'T FORGET SHE HAS HAIR ON HER HEAD, JUST LIKE *ALICE!*

I HAVE AN IDEA!

WE'LL HELP YOU NICK THAT SCEPTER OFF THE QUEEN OF SPADES AGAIN, AND YOU JUST *SWAT* THE QUEEN OF HEARTS ON THE HEAD ONE MORE TIME?

YEAH, AND COMMAND HER TO BE NICE AS PIE FROM NOW ON!

AND REMIND HER THAT SHE AND HER MEANIES AIN'T NOTHIN' BUT A PACK OF CARDS?

AND THEN *YOU'LL* BE QUEEN AND GIVE EVERYBODY FREE TARTS, AND NOT CHOP OUR LITTLE HEADS OFF!

OH, IS THAT THE *QUEEN OF HEARTS* I HEAR OUTSIDE?

IT *IS*! SHE'S COMING UP THE PATH!

!!!

THANK YOU, FEATHER. THEY WERE MAKING ME NERVOUS.

HACK! HACK!

120

♠ I KNOW YOU MUST HAVE MISSED MY HUSBAND AND ME TERRIBLY, AFTER WE WERE THROWN DOWN INTO THAT TREACLE WELL AND FORGOTTEN. ♠

DID I MENTION IT WAS A PAIR OF HEARTS WHO TOSSED US DOWN? ♠

OH, TSK TSK! SUCH A REGRETFUL MISUNDER-STANDING. I MUST HAVE THE GUARDS RESPONSIBLE FOR THE DEED BEHEADED, JUST AS SOON AS I HAVE TIME.

HM. WELL, THERE IS *ANOTHER DECK OF CARDS*, YOU KNOW. WE HAVEN'T HEARD MUCH FROM THEM, BUT THAT ♠ COULD ALWAYS CHANGE...

YOU DON'T MEAN—?

WITH THE OTHER ROYAL PAIRS SAFELY

—I MEAN *SADLY*—

OUT OF COMMISSION, I SUPPOSE IT'S JUST US HEARTS AND SPADES NOW, DEAR...

YES. THE ONE WITH THE SWORDS, AND THE CUPS.

AND WHO KNOWS WHERE THEIR LOYALTIES MIGHT LIE?

THE QUEEN OF HEARTS, SHE'S GIVING ME THE SILENT TREATMENT! SHE MUST REMEMBER ME AND WHAT I DID! IS SHE JUST TOYING WITH ME BEFORE SHE OFFS MY HEAD?

SHE HAS A T-T-TERRIBLY SHORT ATTENTION SPAN, MARY ANN. I'M SURE SHE'S FORGOTTEN ALL ABOUT IT BY NOW.

HUFF HUFF

HER FOCUS IS ALL ON THE QUEEN OF SPADES.

YOU KNOW, MARY ANN... *GASP!* I'M SO VERY GLAD YOU'RE HERE!

WHY, DOES SOMETHING NEED MENDING?

OH, NO, NO, IT'S JUST THAT I WAS SO NERVOUS CAUGHT BETWEEN THE TWO QUEENS *WHEEZE* AND I HAD NO ONE TO TURN TO!

THERE, THERE, MASTER RABBIT. WE'LL MANAGE.

DO YOU KNOW, I HAD A STRANGE CONVERSATION WITH SOME QUEER LITTLE BLOKES WHILE I WAS HANGING ABOUT IN LOOKING-GLASS HOUSE...

THEY BELONG TO THAT ALICE CULT. YOU KNOW, "THE CURIOUS"? THE ONES WHO THINK THE ALICE MONSTER IS SO JOLLY BRILLIANT...

WELL, WITH HER AND HER SHARP TONGUE BEING GONE, THEY SEEM TO WANT *ME* TO BE SOME SORT OF REBEL LEADER, AND STEAL THE CROWN AWAY FROM THE QUEEN OF HEARTS...

I DON'T KNOW WHAT THEY SEE—, IT'S JUST NONSENSE. A SERVING GIRL LIKE ME...

OH, MARY ANN, I THINK YOU'D BE DELIGHTFUL AT REBELLION! IT WOULD BE SO ORDERLY AND TIDY.

THANK YOU, MASTER RABBIT. THAT MEANS A LOT TO ME.

AND DOESN'T EVERY GIRL WANT TO BE A QUEEN OR A PRINCESS?

I HAVE MY DREAMS. LIKE ANY GIRL, I SUPPOSE.

BUT I THINK I *REALLY* JUST WANT TO BE HUMBLE, LITTLE MARY ANN.

WOULD YOU LIKE TO KNOW WHAT THAT VILE SOW DID TO THE OTHER QUEENS?

SHHH! WON'T SHE GET MAD IF YOU TELL ME?

SHE'S TOO BUSY THINKING ABOUT WHAT *SHE'LL* SAY NEXT, SHE'S HARDLY EVEN PAYING ATTENTION TO US.

THE QUEEN OF DIAMONDS AND THE QUEEN OF CLUBS WERE BOTH VAIN, DULL-WITTED CREATURES, AND THE QUEEN OF HEARTS TOOK ADVANTAGE OF THAT.

FIRST SHE WENT TO THE QUEEN OF DIAMONDS...

Our queenly friend,
My ear does bend
To claim your rings are fake!

She snorts and laughs
And says "they're glass."
The Queen of Clubs — that snake!

Then to the
Queen of clubs...

The diamond queen,
She sure is mean.
You ought to hear her talk.

She says your foot
Is clubbed, and that
Explains the way you walk!

MMMMM...

DO YOU SMELL THAT? SOMEBODY'S COOKING SOMETHING TASTY... AND I DON'T BELIEVE WE'VE EATEN SINCE THE HATTER'S BITTER TEA AND STALE CAKES...

FEATHER, COME BACK!

MARY ANN...?

OH, BLAST IT! I'LL CATCH UP IN A BIT!

WELL, COME IN AND SIT DOWN!

129

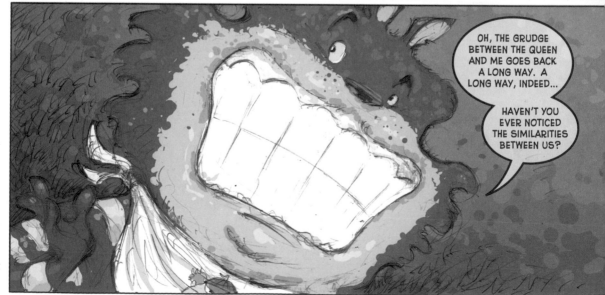

SHE'S MY **SISTER!**

REALLY ?!

WELL, NO. BUT I LIKE TO *THINK* OF HER AS MY SISTER. A TERRIBLE, BULBOUS, OBNOXIOUS SISTER THAT I WISH I WEREN'T RELATED TO...

I'M CONFUSED.

SO WAS I, WHEN I FIRST FOUND OUT!

FOUND OUT THAT SHE *WASN'T* YOUR SISTER?

YES, ARE YOU *SLOW?!* HOW COULD A CAT HAVE A QUEEN FOR A SISTER?!

SERVING GIRL! A LETTER HAS ARRIVED!

YOU ARE WANTED *IMMEDI-ATELY* AT THE ROYAL PALACE.

ALL RIGHT. I'LL BE RIGHT THERE.

WHY CAN'T THOSE DEMANDING QUEENS GIVE THE POOR, EXHAUSTED GIRL A MOMENT'S PEACE? SHE HASN'T SLEPT IN DAYS!

SHE MAY SLEEP ON HER DAY OFF, AND NOT BEFORE.

WELL, THEN?! WHY AREN'T YOU MOVING?

I AM... I'M ALMOST THERE. LOOK, THERE'S THE HEDGE MAZE...

DREAMING IT AND DOING IT ARE TWO ENTIRELY DIFFERENT THINGS!

OH, DUCHY DEAR...

Chapter Six
Cut The Deck!

WHOM ARE YOU TALKING TO?

WHY, *YOU*, MISS! YOU'RE OUR NEW CHAOS QUEEN! GONNA PROTECT US FROM THE MEANIES.

OH, POPPYCOCK! YOU'RE TOUCHED IN THE HEAD, ALL OF YOU!

I WON'T HAVE ANY OF THIS MESSY *CHAOS* ON *MY* SHIFT.

BUT-- BUT ALICE SAID YOU'D HELP GET RID O' THOSE STALE OLD CARDS...

RIGHT! WE WAS HANGING ABOUT IN THE LOOKING-GLASS HOUSE, WHEN SUDDENLY ALICE VANISHED FROM THE MIRROR.

WHEN WE WENT LOOKING FOR HER, WE JUST FOLLOWED SOME SCREAMS AND BANGING ABOUT, AND FOUND 'ER HERE. SHE SAID YOU'D BE A QUEEN OF CHAOS, AND LET EVERYBODY JUST MIND THEIR OWN BUSINESS, EACH TO HIS OWN, LIKE!

NO RULES TO BREAK, NO HEADS TO ROLL! IT'D BE...

NICE.

WHERE IS SHE NOW, THIS BOSSY THING?

WENT OUT LIKE A LIGHT! TALL AS A TREE ONE MINUTE, THEN *POOF*! SHE DISAPPEARED AGAIN. WE LOOKED AROUND, BUT ALL WE FOUND WAS YOU.

YOU JUST REMINDED ME, I WAS HAVING THE FUNNIEST DREAM ABOUT THE ALICE MONSTER. SHE WAS SCATTERING THE QUEENS AND THEIR SOLDIERS ALL ABOUT...

OH!

THE PALACE! HOW DID I GET HERE?

THAT'S AN EXCELLENT QUESTION, MARY ANN.

FEATHER!

YOU'RE ALL... *DIFFERENT*, NOW! JUST *WHAT* DO YOU THINK YOU ARE?

I'M A *SCEPTER*.

NO MORE CLEANING FOR ME!

BLIMEY.

AAAUUUGH!

UNHAND ME, YOU TRAITORS!

OFF WITH YOUR--

SILENCE!

THE KING OF DIAMONDS AND THE KING OF CLUBS! SHE'S BEEN FIXING THE GAME ALL ALONG!

I FOLD.

EXCUSE ME...

PARDON ME, BUT WE ARE THE PEOPLE'S ARMY OF THE CURIOUS, AND WE NAME MARY ANN AS THE NEW QUEEN.

THE CHAOS QUEEN! COME TO SET WONDERLAND FREE FROM YOU... YOU... *BADDIES*!

I THINK NOT, YOU DIRTY LITTLE ANIMALS...

WITH THESE...

THE VOICE SAID YOU'D KNOW WHAT TO DO.

STRANGELY ENOUGH, I GUESS I DO.

THINGS HAVE BECOME CLUTTERED.

IT'S TIME TO...

COME DOWN FROM THERE, YOU SILLY THING!

NO!

MARY ANN, JUST THINK OF THE REGULATIONS YOU COULD IMPOSE...

ALL SUBJECTS MUST WIPE FEET BEFORE ENTERING ANY ABODE! DISHES MUST KEEP THEMSELVES CLEAN AT ALL TIMES OR BE SUBJECT TO FINES AND IMPRISONMENT! ALL ANIMALS, NO MATTER HOW SMALL AND CUTE, MUST WEAR PANTS INDOORS!

WELL, THIS ISN'T EXACTLY WHAT WE HAD IN MIND...

YOU'D NEVER HAVE TO WORK AGAIN...

WELL...

SOME OF THAT DOES SOUND A BIT OF ALL RIGHT...

BUT I DON'T MIND WORKING. AND THERE'S NOTHING DIRTIER THAN POLITICS.

COME ALONG, MASTER RABBIT!

LET'S GO SEE HOW BAD THE DAMAGE IS TO YOUR COTTAGE. I IMAGINE THERE'S LOTS TO DO.

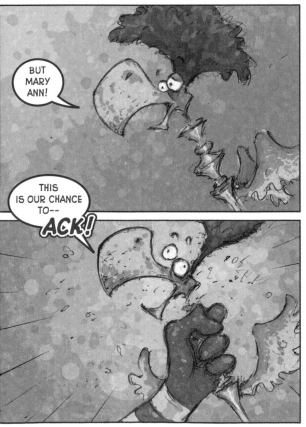

BUT MARY ANN!

THIS IS OUR CHANCE TO-- *ACK!*

WHY SETTLE FOR A DRABBY LITTLE HOUSEMAID QUEEN WHEN YOU CAN HAVE A THOROUGHLY *MAD* KING OF *NONSENSE*?

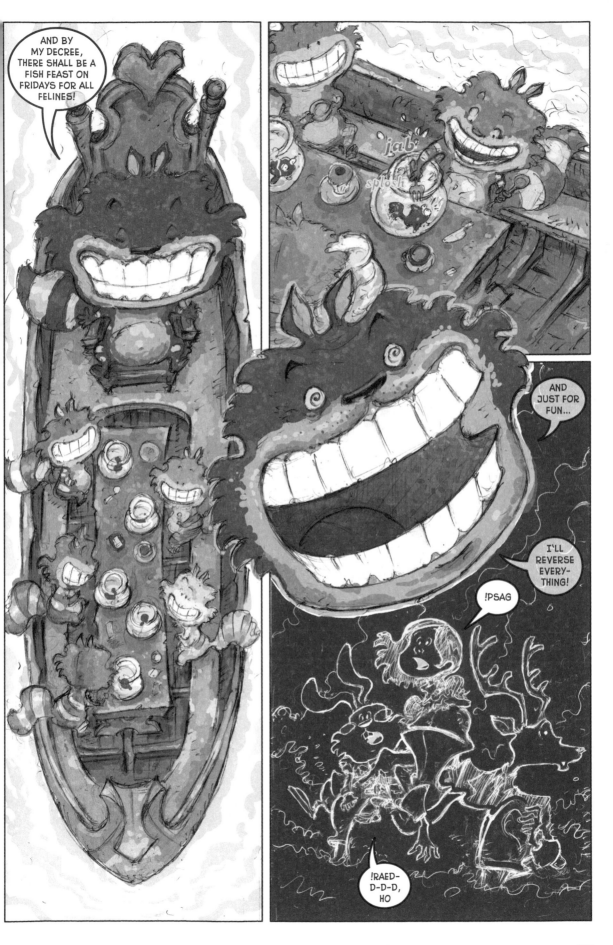

153

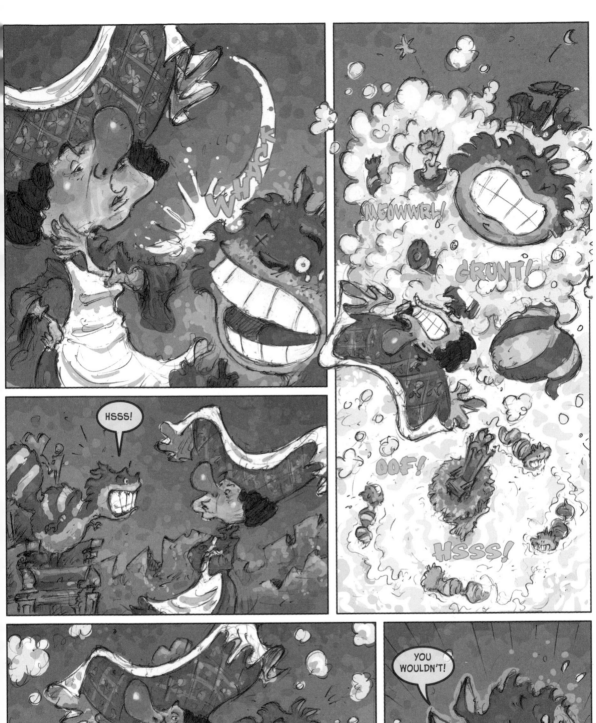

YOU WILL GET DOWN OFF THIS THRONE, OR I SHALL TELL ALL OF YOUR SECRETS!

YOU WOULDN'T!

YOU COULDN'T!

WHO WOULD HAVE THOUGHT THE QUEEN OF HEARTS' SOLDIERS WOULD HAVE SO THOROUGHLY DESTROYED YOUR POOR COTTAGE, MASTER RABBIT?

BUT DON'T WORRY, YOU'LL STAY RIGHT HERE WITH ME UNTIL YOU'RE ON YOUR FEET AGAIN.

EVEN THOUGH I DON'T NORMALLY TAKE IN VAGRANTS, YOU UNDERSTAND.

BUT SEEING AS HOW WE'RE ACQUAINTANCES, I SUPPOSE IT'S ALL RIGHT.

OH, THANK YOU, DEAR!

THESE LITTLE BLOKES WERE SO OBSESSED WITH THAT ALICE MONSTER, BUT THEY SEEM TO HAVE FORGOTTEN ALL ABOUT HER.

OH, WE HAVEN'T FORGOTTEN...

The End.